W9-BYG-093

I Hate My Best Friend

Written and Illustrated by
Ruth Rosner

ANNIE   NINI

Hyperion Books for Children
New York

To Rachael, Tony, and to Marcia Simon.

With special thanks to Kristen Behrens, Ellen Friedman, Lauri London,
Daphne Putka, Sloat Shaw, and Adele Watson

Printed in the United States of America.

First Edition

1 3 5 7 9 10 8 6 4 2

The artwork for each picture is prepared using pencil, gouache, and watercolor.

The book is set in 16-point Berkeley Book.

Library of Congress Cataloging-in-Publication Data

Rosner, Ruth.
I Hate My Best Friend / [written and illustrated by] Ruth Rosner.—1st ed.
p.   cm.
Summary: Annie and Nina are super best friends and do everything
together until Nina's cousin Irina arrives from Russia to live with
the family.
ISBN 0-7868-2079-9 (lib. bdg.)—ISBN 0-7868-1169-2 (pbk.)
[1. Friendship—Fiction. 2. Cousins—Fiction.] I. Title.
PZ7.R71955Su   1997
[Fic]—dc20   96-11478

Table of Contents

ANNIE   NINI

Chapter 1

Slides and Tuna Fish

Her name is Nina, but I call her Nini. She says, "Annie, you are the only one who can call me that because you are my super best friend. Nobody but my super best friend can call me Nini."

Nini and I do everything together. Just the two of us. "Two is the best," says Nini. "Especially when the two is you and me."

Nini is in my class at school. We both

have Mrs. Blue. We secretly call her Mrs. Orange, and we like it best when she wears her hair down without an elastic.

We are in the same reading group. Nini says, "We read out loud with the best best *best* expression. Everybody else is *so* s-l-o-w and b-o-r-i-n-g, if you know what I mean."

We swing on the swings together every day at recess. Nini says, "Nobody can have the horse swings but us. We go the fastest, and the fastest swingers should get the horse swings."

We always eat lunch together. Nini says, "We have the best lunches in the whole school, and anybody who brings anything but peanut butter and raisins is a dumb bunny."

4

We sit at the same table in art. Nini says, "We are the only ones who know how to paint noses. If you make circles for noses or leave them off, you can't be a real artist like we are."

We stand next to each other in the after-school chorus. Nini says, "We sing the loudest, and we sing the best, and we are going to

get the main parts in the spring assembly, that's for sure!"

Nini and I walk home together after school. Nini says, "We have more fun than anybody because I go to your house after school, and you come to my house, and nobody else can come because we are best friends—the best friends on the block, in the town, in the world."

I like being Nini's best friend.

And if sometimes I want to go down the slide at recess or bring tuna fish for lunch, it doesn't matter. Who needs slides or tuna fish anyway? People can live without slides and tuna fish. Swings and peanut butter with raisins are just as good as slides and tuna fish any day.

And then something strange happens.

Chapter 2

Hoarse Rhinoceros

One day at school I say, "Mrs. Orange has red shoes."

Nini says, "Her name is Mrs. Blue and so what?"

I read out loud in my most enormous voice in reading group.

Nini says, "*Shhhhhhhh!*"

I run to save our horse swings at recess.

Nini says, "Only babies play on horse swings."

I take out my peanut butter and raisin sandwich at lunch.

Nini says, "You ought to try something different once in a while, like egg salad."

I practice drawing noses in art.

Nini laughs and says they look like potatoes.

In after-school chorus I sing "Swing Me Up a Little Bit Higher, Obadiah Do" with all my lung power.

Nini holds her ears.

I think maybe Nini will tell me what's wrong on the way home from school, but Nini leaves before I can find her.

I walk home by myself. When I pass

Nini's house, I see Nini playing with some girl with braids I've never seen before.

She doesn't even wave. I pretend that I don't see her.

Then things get worse.

Nini giggles when I read out loud in reading group. She makes faces at me when the teacher isn't looking and gets Nicky and Sarah to giggle, too, even though they are doing workbooks at their desks.

And they giggle some more and point on the way to the cafeteria.

Nini gets permission from the lunch monitor to move to Mary Lou and Janice's table at lunch, even though we barely know Mary Lou and Janice at all. She shares a chair with Mary Lou and eats a bologna sandwich with mustard dripping down the sides.

I eat half of my sandwich and stuff the rest in my coat pocket. We can go out for recess as soon as we're through eating, and I'm the first one out the door.

Even though the horse swing is free, I don't go near it. I sit under a tree at the far end of the playground and fiddle around with some pebbles.

I wonder if Nini sees me sitting by myself. I wish recess would be over.

In art, Nini draws a picture that I know is me because of the barrettes. She makes the hair all ziggy-zaggy and the teeth green.

In after-school chorus I call her a *big dumbhead*. And she calls me a *dumb dodo bird*. She throws me a mean note. It says:

She draws a picture of an old wrinkled rhino wearing my clothes. Broken music flies out of its mouth.

Nini's notes used to make me laugh. But not this time.

I throw her a worse note. It says:

I draw hideous, howling hippos, all with Nini's hair, and then I draw people holding their ears and screaming.

Nini reads the note and looks back at me with her nose pinched and her lips all tight. I stick out my tongue.

She holds her nose and whispers (loudly), "*Oink oink.*"

I yell, "*You stink!*"

Mrs. Blue makes us sit on the side until chorus is over.

"I am *very* surprised," says Mrs. Blue. "I thought you girls were such good friends. Would you like to talk about it?"

Nini shakes her head no. So I shake my head no, too.

Then, when chorus is over, Mrs. Blue says we'll feel better if we both apologize. So I say, *"I'm sorry,"* and Nini says, *"I'm sorry."* But I'm not and I don't think she is, either, because she walks right home without waiting.

I walk home a new way and meet up with Seth and Marika. It's even better than the old way because of the candy store. We all get caramels. Mine has chocolate in the middle.

Chapter 3

The Smell of Peanut Butter

The next day Nini quits after-school chorus. She tells Krista, who tells Aasha, who tells Josh, who tells me. Nini stands right there watching. I stick out my tongue at her. Nini says, "Who cares, silly?"

So I don't play with that old Nini anymore. And I don't bring peanut butter and raisins to school every day. And I do bring tuna fish. And I slide down the slide at recess. And I draw people without noses in art. And I don't care that I have to sing the low part all by myself except for Eric and Andrés in the after-school chorus. And I always walk home with Seth and Marika.

Nini still goes right home after school as fast as she can. Sometimes I see her in the park, but she never looks at me. And she's always with that girl with the braids.

Probably the girl is Nini's new best friend. Probably she calls her Nini. But not me. I call her *Noodlehead*.

I kind of miss Nini a little. Sometimes. Like whenever I smell peanut butter. I wonder if she misses me.

I wonder if old Nini misses our secret whispers. But we don't talk at school at all—not even in reading group.

One day while Mrs. Blue is busy passing out workbooks to the rest of the class, and my group is getting ready to read, Nini picks up the chair next to me and moves it all the way across the circle. "It's too crowded over there," says Nini.

I can feel my face turn so red. I don't even

17

hear Mrs. Blue call on me to read.

"Earth to Annie," says Mrs. Blue.

"Oops," I say. "I must have lost my place. I was thinking about something."

"Would you like to share your thoughts with us?" asks Mrs. Blue.

Actually, I almost want to. I want to say

something out loud to Nini. But I don't really know what it is, so I just shake my head no.

"Then please, Annie," says Mrs. Blue, "begin for us, in your lovely, strong voice, the story on page twenty-five—and be sure to read the title and the name of the author."

I read, but my voice isn't very strong. In fact it is so soft that Mrs. Blue asks me twice to try it louder. And she has to tell me three times how to pronounce "epitome." She ends my turn after only one page.

Nini gets to read three pages. She reads with so much expression that everybody claps. Except me.

In the afternoon, we have to build pyramids with a partner. Marika is home with the flu, so Seth asks me if I'll work with him.

I'm surprised that Nini doesn't have a

partner. "I'm lucky," says Nini loudly, "because I get to be partners with Mrs. Blue."

When I get home from school that afternoon, my mother says, "How come we never hear from Nini anymore? I never have to chase you girls off the phone these days!"

"We're too busy," I say. "We don't have one second to call each other."

My mother nods her head. I know she knows something is the matter because she gives me that I'm-so-sorry look and bakes homemade chocolate-chip cookies instead of going to the store to get the kind in the packages that we usually get. "Tomorrow we can get art supplies," she says.

"I think I'm playing with Seth and Marika," I say. But I don't. We all walk home together, as usual, but I say, "See you tomorrow," when we get to my house.

Chapter 4

Are They Staying Forever?

And then one day at recess something surprising happens. I accidentally wave to Nini—I guess because I catch her catching me staring.

"What are you looking at, *Annie Turkey Face?*" she says.

"Your dress, *Nini Cowhead*," I say. "I was looking at those red ruffles."

"It's dumb," she says. "My mother made

me wear it. It's just like the one she got for my cousin."

"What cousin?" I ask.

"Irina from Russia," she says.

"Does she have braids?" I ask.

Nini nods. "Her whole family moved to our house. But she goes to some other school. Nobody speaks Russian at our school. But they do at hers. Even the signs on the doors are in Russian."

"Are they staying forever?" I ask.

"Nobody told me," says Nini. "We'll probably have to spend the whole summer together. They just might stay forever and ever. I bet they do.".

Nini puts her hands on her hips like she does when she's annoyed. "You're lucky," she says. "You don't have any cousins you don't know moving into your room and into your clothes. You never have to do anything you don't want to do."

Then she turns and races off to the swing set. I run and run until I catch up with her. "I miss you at after-school chorus," I say. "I hate singing the low part all by myself with all those boys."

"I have better things to do now," says Nini, "with my cousin."

"You said you didn't like her," I say. "You said I was lucky I didn't have any cousins moving into my house."

"I changed my mind," says Nini.

"I bet she doesn't like to swing on horse swings," I say.

Nini looks at me funny. "No, she doesn't," she says. "She likes tire swings. And she doesn't like peanut butter, either, so my mom forgets to get it at the store. And I can't stay for singing because I have to keep her company after school and help her with her English."

"You do?" I ask. "That must be fun. Wish I could do something like that."

"You do?" asks Nini.

Then she says, "I really miss peanut butter and raisins on that gushy bread you used to have."

"We mainly have tuna fish now," I say, "but we still have that bread if you want to come over ever and have some."

Then Mrs. Blue blows the whistle and recess is over. Nini runs to the front of the line. I almost start to run with her, but I take my time.

I'd really like to meet her cousin. Even if she is a pain. I've never met anyone who speaks Russian.

"I'm walking home with Seth and Marika after school," I say when Nini plops down beside me in art. "Come join us, if you like. We go home a new way."

"Sorry," says Nini. "I have to go straight home because of . . ." Nini's voice drops to a whisper. "Because of what I told you about my cousin. Bring me a peanut butter sandwich tomorrow, okay, Annie?"

I guess she forgot that I mainly bring tuna fish.

That night I dream that Nini is flying around my head. I'm making peanut butter sandwiches on gigantic pieces of bread, and Nini scoops them up as soon as I throw on

the raisins. *"Fantastically delicious!"* she shouts. *"Best in the world!"*

I forget all about Nini's sandwich the next morning. But that's all right. I see her take out a cheese and tomato sandwich and a cup of pudding at lunch.

That afternoon, Nini borrows my pencil in reading group and whispers to me about the new girl. "I can't believe she wears those white ankle socks!" says Nini.

I nod even though I don't really care if she wears white ankle socks. Maybe everything else was in the wash. I should say that, but then Nini says, "Isn't it great being best friends again?"

Before I can open my mouth or even think of what to say, Nini is raising her hand to read.

28

After school, Nini calls her mother on the pay phone to see if she can walk home with Seth and Marika and me. I guess her mother says no, because I see her face drop as if she's about to cry.

Then, in an instant, she is running down the hall and through the double doors shouting, "Not today! *Hasta la vista!* See ya tomorrow!"

I kind of feel sorry for her. I figure this has a lot to do with her cousin.

That night, my mother talks to her mother on the phone. I hear my mother say, "The girls really do miss each other." And then she nods and says, "Uh-huh . . . uh-huh . . . okay . . . I see . . . I see . . . that's right! Absolutely! Yes, yes!"

The next thing I know, Nini and I have an after-school play date at Nini's house.

Chapter 5

The One in the Middle

Nini's mother and Irina pick us up in the station wagon.

"Everybody in the back!" says Nini's mother.

Nini and I used to play hearts in the back and sing Beatles songs. Nini's mother loves the Beatles (though *my* mother thinks they're not half as great as the Rolling Stones).

I don't imagine we'll play hearts or sing "We all live in a yellow submarine!" anymore.

I don't know what games they play in Russia or even one Russian song.

I feel very quiet and don't know what I'm going to say.

I'm worried that Irina will be a real pain. After all, she gives Nini such a hard time. I hope she doesn't whine.

"Hi!" says Irina. "You are my cousin Nina's best friend! I am very glad to meet with you!" Then she gives me a big hug.

She doesn't whine one time on the way home, and she knows all the verses to "Yellow Submarine."

"I taught her," says Nini. "I taught her to play hearts, too." ("But I win most of the time," Nini whispers to me.)

We have time to play one game of hearts in the car, because Nini's mother has to stop

at the market to pick up a chicken. Irina
beats both of us.

("Nini lets me win," Irina whispers to me.)

I nod. I pretend to agree, but it's easy to
see that Irina is a quick learner. She can play
a mean game of hearts.

And then we're at Nini's house. We all go arm in arm up the walk. "I get to be the one in the middle," says Nini, squeezing in between Irina and me.

So here we are—friends again. Except we don't play together every day after school.

I go over to Nini's house on Wednesdays. We help Irina learn English. Sometimes we just talk. Sometimes we tell stories.

Sometimes Nini and Irina come over to my house on Saturdays. Nini says, "Let's play school!"

Everybody wants to be Mrs. Orange and wear the long skirt and have long hair.

Irina doesn't even need the wig. Her hair is the longest when she takes down her braids.

Last Saturday, Nini said, "I wish Mrs. Orange would cut her hair. Then my hair would be perfect."

On the day of the spring assembly, Irina comes with Nini to hear me sing.

"Next year, we'll sing our own song together," says Nini. "We'll be louder and better than anybody."

Irina says, "You sang abso-*luuute*-ly beautiful."

I say, "Spa-*see*-ba." In Russian, that means "thanks."

When Nini finally gets permission to move back to our old table at lunch, she gives me a funny look.

I think she's surprised to see Seth and Marika there, too. "Isn't it a little crowded?" asks Nini when Seth puts his juice glass with

the special straw on the top of her lunch box.
("I thought they'd move," she whispers.)

"We can work it out," I say.

Seth wants the four of us go outside
together for recess. We are just the right
number for jump rope and four square.
But when everybody's eating and talking

together, Nini whispers to me, "Want to play just by ourselves?"

"Not today, Nini," I whisper back. "I really want to play four square."

Chapter 6

The Monster Ogress

This afternoon when I go over Nini's house I get a brainstorm.

"Who wants to put on a play?" I ask. "This great idea flew into my head when Mrs. Blue—"

"Orange!" interrupts Nini. "We call her Mrs. Orange."

"Anyhow," I go on, "when she cleaned out Colin's desk and found all that stuff in there and said, 'You are a real pack rat, Colin! In all my years of teaching, I never saw such a hoard! Have you been walking through the universe, picking up everything in sight?'"

"He was so embarrassed!" says Nini. "I wish I could have some of those action figures, and that yo-yo."

"So I got this idea," I went on. "You see, there's this ogress—really gigantic—who steals treasures from everybody's house, and she has this enormous collection of couches and refrigerators and televisions and pianos and potatoes and cars and even trees she pulls up by the roots and shoes and everything. And she keeps it all in a mess in her gigantic house."

"And then this beautiful princess comes along," says Nini. "I could play her—and the

ogress wants to capture her, but, instead, the princess captures the ogress and all her stuff and . . ."

"Puts it all in large museum," says Irina.

"THE large museum," says Nini.

"She puts it all in THE large museum," repeats Irina. "Like in Russia, like . . . THE Hermitage, where I go with my father, because they do not know who is THE owner of THE stuff!"

"No! No!" says Nini. "The ogress captures the princess and locks her up and then decides to capture all the princesses in the world, except—and this is the exciting part—the main princess (that's me) escapes and gets a couple of kings and queens to help her capture the ogress and put her in a dark, wet, underground dungeon.

"All she gets to eat all day is tuna fish and stale blini. And then the princess and a prince and some of the kings and queens live in the ogress's big old house and split up the

43

stuff or sell it or something and buy a space
module and the princess drives it straight to
the moon."

"Let's get started!" I say. "And we could

44

call Seth and Marika and they could be in it, too."

Nini makes a face. "We don't need anybody else for our play. It's a three-actor play, not a five-actor play. And we're the best actors! We can do all the parts!"

If we were at my house, I'd call Seth and Marika. I think we really need a bigger cast. But we're at Nini's house so I let her do it her way. "Who wants to be the ogress?" I ask.

"I'm the princess, remember?" says Nini.

"I can be it!" says Irina. "I can be THE monster ogress!" She scrunches up her face and snarls. She grabs pillows and cushions off the couch and dumps them on the floor.

"Mine!" she shouts. "MINE! MINE! MINE!"

She dances wildly around the pillows and cushions. She stomps and she stamps and she throws herself on top of them.

"Bravo!" I shout. "Encore! Encore!" Irina was spectacular.

"My mother doesn't like shoes on the furniture!" snaps Nini.

I say, "Irina, you are absolutely going to be a great actress."

Nini says, "Well, *I'm* going to be a great movie star. Greater than Greta Garbo and Ginger Rogers."

"Well, then," I say, "Miss Gina Lollobrigida. If you win an Oscar, you'd better thank me in your speech like this: 'And I wish to give greatest and most humble heartfelt thanks to my oldest and most wonderful

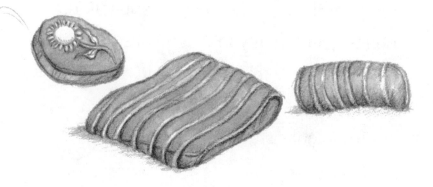

friend, Annie, who made up the play about the ogress and started the whole thing.'"

"I thought up the part about the princess," says Nini. "She's the *star* of the whole thing."

"I think the big ogress is star, so, you thank me, also." Irina laughs.

"You're laughing at me!" says Nini. "Stop laughing . . . and it's '*theeeeee* star!' And . . . and . . . you know what else? You fly over here in some plane from Russia and you barge into my room and you take all my things and you make me help you talk better English, and then you laugh your head off at me! You *are* a big ogress and I wish you would *just . . . get . . . LOST!*"

Irina looks stunned.

Nini glares.

I want to disappear.

All I think of to do is put my arm around Irina and say, "She doesn't really mean it, Rini."

"Oh, super great! Now she's 'Rini,'" says you know who.

So, Irina bursts into tears, Nini runs up to her room and slams the door, and I think it's time for me to go home. But Nini's mother comes into the picture and sort of saves the day.

"Girls!" she shouts. "And that means you, too, Nina-pie, up there in your room!"

Nini sticks her head out the door. I can see her from the bottom of the stairs. Her face is all red. Irina is sitting on the floor in the middle of the pillows, sobbing.

"I have treats for all of you," says her mother, "*if* the three of you can get along the way I know you can and give each other a nice hug, and *if* you can put those cushions and pillows back where they belong on the couch like the thoughtful people I know you are."

I hate it when Nini's mother calls us "people." She always does that when she's really angry, even though she sounds as cool as a cucumber.

So Nini—who has always loved treats better than anything, for as long as I can remember—flies down the stairs.

And we all hug and say we're sorry, even though I'm not sure what I did, and I feel sorry for Irina and extremely annoyed at

Nini, who ruined the afternoon and the play.

Then Nini's mother gives us each a beautiful box of colored pencils and a thick pad of white paper to draw on. And we sit at the table and draw pictures for the rest of the afternoon.

"It was fabulous good play idea, Annie," says Irina when it's time for me to go. "We do it next time."

"Remember, *I'm* the princess," says Nini.

How could I forget?

Chapter 7

What? Nothing.

The following day at school, we have a substitute, who lets us all do a project. Free choice.

Seth and Marika and I build a whole scene from the ogress story. We ask Nini to help, but she says she is much too busy doing her own story.

This afternoon when we're walking out the door to go home, Nini grabs my jacket and starts to pull me down the hall. *"Super best friends!"* she shouts loud enough for everybody to hear.

"Turkey Face, Noodlehead!" I holler.

"Cowhead, Dum-dum!" Nini hollers back, laughing. She keeps on laughing so hard. "We kid around better than anybody, Annie.

Nobody in the whole world kids around better than we do."

I just look at her. "Marika's a pretty good kidder," I say. "So is Seth. And you know, that Irina's a *really* good kidder."

Nini looks at me funny. "I have to go," she says. "My mother's taking me and Irina to get *all* the ice cream we can eat. Nobody else can come! It's *cousins only*."

"*Nini!*" I say.

"What?" she says.

"Nothing," I say. "I really have to go, too. See you later, alligator."

Then I run off as fast as I can go. I know if I hurry, I'll catch up with Seth and Marika at the candy store.

And I do.

If you liked *I Hate My Best Friend*, look for these books in your library or bookstore:

The Best, Worst Day by Bonnie Graves
Lucy wants Maya, the new girl in her class with curly brown hair and pierced ears, to be her best friend, but how can Lucy get her attention?

Jenius: The Amazing Guinea Pig by Dick King-Smith
Judy is sure that Jenius, her prodigious guinea pig, will stun her class at show-and-tell . . . as long as Jenius is smart enough to stay away from scary cats.

Jennifer, Too by Juanita Havill
Can Jennifer prove she's as sneaky a spy, as scary a ghost-story teller, and as brave a knight as any boy on the block?

Mystery of the Tooth Gremlin by Bonnie Graves
Jesse is excited about losing his first tooth, but when he leaves it on his desk, it mysteriously disappears.

No Room for Francie by Maryann Macdonald
With six siblings, Francie never has her own space, so how will she produce the private clubhouse she's planned?

Solo Girl by Andrea Davis Pinkney
With the help of her brothers, Bud and Jackson, Cass may finally get her chance to be friends with the Fast Feet Four, the best double-Dutch jumpers on the block.

Spoiled Rotten by Barthe DeClements
The second-grade teacher will not tolerate Andy's spoiled-rotten attitude; will his best friend, Scott, stand up for him in front of their classmates?

Read all the Hyperion Chapters

Ruth Rosner

In between second and third grade, I moved, changed schools, and left behind my best friend, Linda. I still got to see her on Tuesdays and Saturdays, though. My favorite sandwich was—and still is—tuna fish, but I also ate peanut butter and egg salad. At my new school, I met a girl who ate egg salad that had shells in it—her mother said it was healthier that way! When I grew up I wanted to be a singer-dancer but instead I became an author-illustrator.